DÚN LAO... ...FROM
L... ...HDOWN COUNTY
...RY STOCK

The Great Green Monster

by

Maggie Pearson

Illustrated by Jotter Studio

To Liberty, Jake, Jonathan, Jessica and Iona. With thanks for their help.

First published in 2009 in Great Britain by
Barrington Stoke Ltd
18 Walker St, Edinburgh, EH3 7LP

www.barringtonstoke.co.uk

Copyright © 2009 Maggie Pearson
Illustrations © Jotter Studio

The moral right of the author has been asserted in accordance with the Copyright, Designs and Patents Act 1988

ISBN: 978-1-84299-636-2

Printed in Great Britain by Bell & Bain Ltd

Contents

Chapter 1
The Monster

What kind of a monster was it?

That's hard to say.

What did it look like?

That's hard to tell. Most people were running away from it too fast to take a proper look. The slow ones only saw it from the inside.

It must have been pretty small to begin with, or it never could have got through that gap between the rocks. That gap was the only way in and out of the valley.

Slithering between the rocks it came, into that lush, green valley.

Some parts of Africa are dry and dusty. The sun beats down and it never rains, so nothing grows. In other places the trees grow so thick, the sun never reaches the ground. So nothing much grows there either. Here in the valley, the sun shone just right and the rain fell, but not too often. There were trees, but not too many. There was fresh water and grass for the cows and goats to feed on. Enough land left over to grow a few crops too.

Paradise!

Till that green, greedy monster wiggled its way in.

That monster was hungry.

Soon the hunters began to notice that there weren't so many animals about as there were before. Not so many deer, antelope or gazelle. Nowhere near so many zebras or giraffes or wild pigs.

Very soon, none at all.

Not so much as a rabbit.

Of course the women didn't believe the hunters when they came back with nothing. No meat for the pot!

"You just didn't look hard enough," the women said.

"You men!" the women said. "You've been lazing about out there all day while we've been cleaning and washing and looking after the children and weeding the vegetable patch. Well, it's vegetable stew for dinner again. I'm not killing another chicken."

Then some chickens went missing.

"Who's stolen my chickens?" said Old Man Misery. You know the sort. There's someone like him in every village, every street; never happy, always moaning.

"Which one of you stole my chickens?" yelled Old Man Misery.

The others told him, "Nobody's stolen your chickens, old man."

"Why would we steal your chickens?" they asked him. "We've got enough chickens of our own."

"They've just wandered off, the way chickens do," someone said.

"They'll be back," said his wife.

But Old Man Misery's chickens didn't come back.

Nor did the dog that ran off barking, into the night. Barking at shadows, the way dogs do.

That was the same night some pigs went missing, right close by.

Soon after that, a goat.

A small girl called Abi was sent to look for the goat. She knew she'd be in big trouble if she didn't find it. So she looked harder than the rest of them. Harder than the men when they went out hunting. Harder even than Old Man Misery looking for his chickens.

Abi could hear the goat but though she looked and looked she couldn't see it anywhere.

The sound was coming from the other side of a small hill. She walked round to the other side of the hill. No goat there. Just the sound of it bleating, back in the place where she'd come from. So she walked on, back to where she began.

Still no goat. She could still hear it bleating. That goat must be inside the hill.

How had it got itself in there? Was there a cave that she hadn't seen? Come to think of it, she'd never seen a hill there before.

Abi stood and she thought and she stared at the hill which wasn't there before. An odd sort of hill it was, smooth and green, but without any grass on it. One side of it snaking away, almost like a tail. On the other side was what looked almost like a head. There were its ears. There was its nose. There were its eyes!

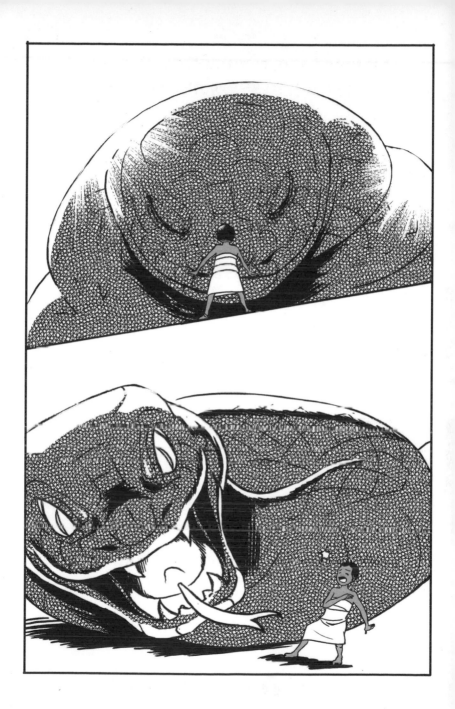

Two big eyes staring at her from the side of a hill that wasn't there before.

And a mouth. A great, red mouth yawning wider and wider, till it was wide enough to swallow her up.

Chapter 2
Hunger

Abi ran!

Ran, ran, ran as fast as her plump little legs would carry her, all the way back to the village. "There's a great big thing out there!" she cried.

"What sort of a thing?" the people asked.

"A monster!" Abi cried.

"A monster?" they said. "What sort of a monster?"

Abi shook her head. "I don't know."

"What did it look like?" her mother asked.

"Big and green! Big as a hill! Big enough to swallow our goat! Swallow it right up! It looked like it was going to swallow me too," said Abi.

They shook their heads.

"There's no such thing, little girl," the hunters said.

"You're making it up," said Abi's mother.

"You're telling stories," said Abi's father, "because you can't find that goat you lost. How would a monster that big ever get into our valley, through that narrow gap between the rocks?"

"All the same," said one of the hunters, "maybe we should take a look."

So they went, taking their spears and arrows and hunting knives with them, just in case.

But spears and arrows and knives were no use against that great, green, greedy monster. All they did was make it itch. They made it angry!

It swallowed the first hunter head first.

The rest watched his feet vanish down the monster's throat. Then they all turned round to run.

Slithering after them the monster came, faster than any man could go. One by one it swallowed them up.

Back in the village, the women and children and the old folk waited and waited, but none of the hunters came back.

That monster was still hungry.

It ate up all the dogs, the goats, the cows and the pigs.

The more it ate, the more hungry it grew.

It ate the women and the children and the old folk and Abi too.

Creeping out of the shadows it came, when they were sleeping. Attacking in broad day-light when they were getting water from the river or working in the fields. Till there was nobody left in all that lush, green valley, but one woman and her new-born baby.

How did she get away?

This one, she was smarter than the rest. She covered herself with ash from the fire till she was grey all over, grey as a rock. When the monster came by, she didn't scream and run. She curled herself up with her baby – "Hush, little baby!" she said, "Don't cry," – beside a heap of cow dung. She kept herself still as a rock.

She was smart and she was lucky. The monster's eye-sight wasn't too good. *What was that over there? Just another old grey rock,* it thought.

What was that smell? it thought. Could it be man-meat?

It sniffed again. Came closer. Sniffed harder.

The woman kept still, still as a rock. The baby didn't cry.

Closer the monster came and closer.

Sniff – sniff – sniff! *Nothing there after all but a heap of cow dung*, the monster thought.

So off it went, to find another valley with more meat to feed on, slithering down the narrow path between the rocks, the same way it came in.

And got itself well and truly stuck.

The more it ate the more hungry it had grown. The more it ate, the fatter. It had eaten so much and grown so fat it couldn't go forward, couldn't wiggle back.

So there it had to stay, waiting till it grew thin again, sleeping and dreaming sweet dreams of the next lush green valley, full of deer, antelopes, gazelles, zebras, giraffes, wild pigs and rabbits, chickens, goats, dogs, cows and – best of all – man-meat!

Chapter 3
Growing Up Fast

Back in the village, the woman and her baby lay very still for a long, long time. There wasn't a sound or a sign of life anywhere, only a few birds flying high above and the odd splash from the crocodile pool. Oh, yes, there were still crocodiles. Even that great green monster had to draw the line somewhere.

When the woman was sure the monster wasn't coming back, she went down to the river to wash away the ashes and the cow-dung, leaving her baby behind, sleeping under a bit of old deer skin.

She wasn't gone more than five minutes. Maybe ten, then – but no more.

When she came back, what did she find? No baby, but a fine young boy standing there. Straight-backed, bright-eyed and a smile on him you could slip a slice of melon into, sideways on. All he was dressed in was a bit of old deer skin.

"Who are you?" she said. "Where's my baby? What have you done with him?"

"I am your baby."

She saw that that bit of deer skin tied round his waist was the same bit of deer skin she'd left her baby sleeping under.

It must be something he ate, the woman thought. *You turn your back for a moment! But that's babies for you. They'll chew on anything that comes to hand.*

"I don't know what you've been chewing on while I've been gone," she said. "But don't you eat any more of it. Or you'll be an old man by evening and dead by morning."

"What's evening?" he said. He was still just a baby, after all, born that very morning.

"Wait and see," she said.

"What's old? What's dead?"

"You'll see for yourself, all in good time. Go out and play now," his mother said.

So out he went, walking through the village, looking for someone to play with. He peered into all the houses. *Why were they empty? What were the houses for, if not for people to live in? So where were all the people?*

"Where are all the people?" he asked his mother.

"They went away," she said.

"All of them?"

"All of them."

"Where did they go?" he asked her. "Why did they go away?"

"You ask too many questions. Off you go and play now. I've got to get the dinner on."

He was going to ask her, "What's for dinner?" But she had this look in her eye that mothers get sometimes. He knew the answer would be, "Wait and see!"

So off he went again and he found a spear. It had been dropped by one of the hunters when he was running away from the monster.

"What's this?" he asked his mother when he got back home.

"That's a spear," she said.

"What's it for?"

She shook her head. "You don't want to know."

"Yes I do," the boy said.

It didn't take him long to work out for himself what the spear was for. There's not much you can do with a spear but stab or slash or throw it at things. He played with it for a bit outside then he called to his mother to show her what he could do.

"Watch me! Watch me! See me hit that tree-stump over there. I can hit it every time now. It's a fine spear. Where did it come from? Who did it belong to? Why did he leave it lying there when he went away?"

So many questions!

"If you don't stop asking so many questions," his mother said, "that great, green, greedy monster's going to come back and swallow you right up!" Oh! What had she said?

"Monster!" he said. "What monster?"

Another question!

"The one that ate your father and all the rest of them. And after it's swallowed you it's going to come back and eat me," she said. "Then you'll be sorry."

"I won't let it eat you," the boy said.

"How are you going to stop it? You'll be inside it already."

"Then I'll shout and I'll kick and I'll dance! I'll give that monster such a pain, it'll spit me out again. Then I'll save you. Is dinner ready?"

"You see the sun up there? When the sun dips down between those two hills over there, that's when dinner will be ready. Then you'll see what evening looks like."

So off he went, to watch the sun go down and find out what evening looked like.

Chapter 4
Fight of the Century

What his mother didn't know was that that great, green, greedy monster was still trapped there in that gap between the hills. So there wasn't a gap, only something that looked like another hill in the way. It was spoiling his view of the sun going down. So the boy climbed up the hill so he could get a better look at the sky. An odd sort of hill it was. It was as hard as rock under his feet but the colour of it was like soft, green grass. He bent down and touched it. It was warm. And it was moving slowly up and down, up and down, as if the hill was breathing.

He ran down the far side and turned to look at this hill that wasn't like any other hill he'd seen. But then, what did he know? He was less than one day old.

The monster felt a tickling in places that were hard to scratch. An itch at the end of its nose.

It opened one eye, then the other. And saw a boy, straight-backed, bright-eyed and with a smile on him you could slip a slice of melon into, side-ways on.

"I know who you are!" yelled the boy. "You're the monster that wants to eat my mother. And I'm the one that's going to stop you! Wait here. I'll be back!"

With one spring he jumped up onto its nose, ran up its head and down the other

side, along its back and its long snaky tail and away.

The monster was left itching from nose to tail, and it still couldn't scratch.

"I've found it! I've found it!" he told his mother.

"Found what?" she said.

"That monster you told me about. Where's that spear I found?"

"You don't need a spear," she said. "Sit down and eat your dinner."

"I can't kill it with my bare hands."

"You can't kill it with a spear. Your father tried and where is he now? Inside that monster's belly with all the rest of them. Besides, your dinner's ready."

"Keep it warm," he said. "I'll be back."

Off he went, running down the path, with his spear in his hand. Stabbing and jabbing and throwing it ahead.

The monster was in a really bad mood by now. The first two lots of itching had only just worn off. Now here it came again! A pattering of feet from the tip of its tail to the tip of its nose. Still no way to scratch the itch! It was that boy again.

I will eat him! I will! thought the monster. I'll start slimming tomorrow.

It lifted its head and it roared.

The boy danced and laughed and shook his spear. "Come on then, if you think you're hard enough!"

The monster lunged with its head. It was the only bit of it that wasn't stuck fast between the rocks.

The boy sprang back, laughing. "Missed me!"

The monster roared again.

The boy pulled a face. "Phew! Your breath smells terrible!"

The monster lunged again.

This time the boy didn't jump back. He jabbed with his spear. Jabbed with all his strength. It was like hitting solid rock.

Then began the fight of the century!

On one side the monster. Think of the size of it! Think of all those people and animals it had eaten, all piled up together inside its belly! That's how big it had grown.

Against the monster a boy, new-born that morning. Armed with a spear, it's true. But the jab of a spear was like being pricked by a pin for the monster. An insect bite, that itched like mad and drove it wild.

The boy kept on jabbing and stabbing, looking for a weak spot. He was less than a day old but in his bones he knew there had to be a weak spot.

In the end it was the itching that did it. The need to scratch. The monster kept wiggling and jiggling itself against the rocks. Maybe it had lost weight, just a little. It was almost a day since it had had anything to eat. It wiggled and jiggled some more. Maybe it had lost weight, just enough.

Just enough to get one stubby front leg free!

The monster swiped at the boy. But he was ready. He danced away.

"Come on, you old monster! Catch me if you can!"

He'd seen the weak spot, underneath, where the stubby leg joined the body. The skin was paler, softer there.

He jabbed again with his spear.

"Come on, you old monster! Come on! Come on!"

The monster swiped again. Again the boy danced out of the way. Jabbed again.

Jab – swipe – missed!

Jab – swipe – missed again!

Each time the boy edged closer.

Closer still. So close! So very close!

The monster swiped again, going for the kill – and the boy took his chance, aiming for that weak spot where the leg joined the body.

And the spear struck deep into the monster's chest and through its heart.

Slowly, slowly that great, green, greedy monster toppled over and lay still.

Chapter 5
Brave Boy

The monster was dead. Stone dead, no question about it.

So why was its belly rumbling?

It sounded as if the monster was talking to itself, deep down inside.

Talking in all sorts of different voices.

First an old woman: "What was all that about?"

Then a man: "Search me, but I'm glad it's over. I feel quite seasick."

"How would you know?" A third voice joined in. "You've never been to sea."

"Never even seen it." That was the old woman again.

"I've heard stories," said the man's voice.

"Shh! All of you." That sounded like another woman. "I'm trying to listen. It's gone very quiet out there."

"Too quiet, if you ask me," someone else said.

After that the boy lost count. They were all talking at once.

"I wonder what's going on."

"Not much, by the sound of it."

"Hang on. There's a hole here. I can see day-light."

"Let's take a look."

"You wait your turn."

"What can you see?"

"A boy."

"Anyone we know?"

"I don't think so."

"Does it matter? Maybe he can get us out of here. Help!"

"Help!"

"All together now – help!"

"Help!" they all shouted.

"You, boy, help us! Get us out of here."

The boy didn't need telling twice. He set to work to make the hole bigger – slashing and hacking with his spear – a knife would have been better, but he didn't think to run home for one.

The sight of all those people crawling out of the monster's belly! Blinking in the last of the day-light. Sniffing themselves – phew! They smelt terrible! But they didn't care.

"Thank you, boy!" they said.

"Thank you!"

"Who are you, boy?" an old man asked.

"Where did you come from?" asked Abi. You remember Abi, the small girl who found the monster.

"What's your name?" they asked him.

"My name?" said the boy. "I don't know. I was only born today. I don't think my mother's had time to think of a name yet."

They were all full of ideas then.

"Hero-boy?"

"Super-boy!"

"Boy-sent-to-save-us-from-the-great-green-greedy-monster?"

"Boy-who-was-not-afraid?"

"Akim – that means brave boy."

"That'll do," he said. "You can call me Akim if you want." He just wanted to be off home for his dinner.

They carried Akim up on their shoulders back to the village, everyone laughing and

singing together. The dinner was spoilt but his mother couldn't be cross with him. Not when she saw all the people she thought she'd never see again, all laughing and dancing and clapping their hands and singing the praises of her boy who was only born that morning.

After the people came the animals from out of the monster's belly; the goats, dogs, cows, pigs and chickens – all but a few of Old Man Misery's chickens, which the monster had eaten first. It had swallowed the other animals so fast it hadn't had time to digest them.

Old Man Misery limped along, moaning as always. "Look what that boy's done to my leg!"

"You shouldn't have got in the way, old man, when Akim was cutting us out of that monster's insides."

"Look at it!" moaned Old Man Misery. "It's dripping blood. Stupid boy! Why couldn't he be more careful!"

"Stop moaning, old man," they said. "We're alive. That's the main thing."

"Can't you be happy just to be alive?" said Abi.

Old Man Misery wasn't happy. He never was. "He might at least say sorry," he grumbled.

Chapter 6
Playing Tricks

Akim didn't say he was sorry, not that day, nor any day afterwards. Instead Akim made things worse, limping round the village, pretending he was Old Man Misery, calling out, "Oh, my chickens! Oh, my leg! Oh, my poor leg! Oh, my poor, poor chickens!" Everyone laughed.

Soon all his friends were doing it too, whenever Old Man Misery showed his face:

"Oh, my chickens!" they moaned. "Oh, my poor leg!"

They drove Old Man Misery wild. But he could never catch them.

Sometimes our boy would hide in the bush near Old Man Misery's house and make chicken noises.

Old Man Misery would go limping off into the bush hoping to find that his chickens had come home again. Not eaten by the monster after all.

Then he'd hear them laughing, running off, our boy and all his friends. Old Man Misery shaking his stick at them.

Old Man Misery made up his mind not to keep chickens any more. He told his wife to kill the rest and make them into a stew for his dinner.

"All of them?" she said.

"All of them," said Old Man Misery.

"In one big stew?" his wife asked.

"In one big stew," he said.

So she killed all the chickens, made them into one big stew and set the stew over the fire to cook. Off she went to weed the vegetable patch.

After a while Akim came walking by and smelt that stew. The smell of that stew was something wonderful! Snores were coming from the house where Old Man Misery was taking a nap. His wife was busy weeding the vegetable patch.

So Akim took the lid off the pot and tasted that stew. The taste of it was more than wonderful! He was a growing boy and he was hungry. And his mother had told him he must always eat up what was put in front of him. Every scrap. So he did. Akim ate every scrap of that chicken stew. Nothing left but a pile of chicken bones.

Old Man Misery was still snoring. Soon he'd be awake and yelling for his dinner.

What did Akim do then? He put the chicken bones back in the pot. Then he stirred in a heap of cow-dung till the pot was full to the brim again. Akim put the lid back on and hid in the bush so he could see Old Man Misery's face when he took his first taste of his chicken dinner.

And when he did – "Must have been your sour face that did it, old man!" yelled the boy. "Your face is enough to turn any good stew to cow-dung!"

Off he ran through the village, limping, yelling, "Oh, my poor leg! Oh, my chickens! Oh, my dinner!"

Everyone laughed, knowing he'd played another trick on Old Man Misery. Poor old man! They felt sorry for him, but they couldn't help laughing.

Old Man Misery, he'd had enough. He watched which way Akim went one day. Old Man Misery dug a deep hole in the path Akim would have to take when he came back.

Deep enough to sprain an ankle. Maybe even break a leg. "Let's see how he likes walking with a limp!" muttered Old Man Misery.

He went on digging away, deeper and deeper, beginning to wonder if he might be over-doing things a bit.

What if he breaks his neck too? he wondered. Why, then, I'll dance on his grave!

He covered the hole with sticks and grass. He would have liked to stay and watch.

Instead he went off home for his dinner. He didn't want anyone to know he was the one who'd dug that hole.

Time went by.

Evening came.

Along came Akim, on his way home for dinner. Straight down the hole he fell, sticks and grass tumbling around him. Feeling a bit surprised as he fell to find a hole there. There was no hole there that morning.

He was even more surprised when he hit the bottom with a bit of a thump – and went on falling. He fell right through the bottom of the hole Old Man Misery had dug.

Down, down, down he fell. No one ever fell this far before and lived.

No one till now.

Chapter 7
The One-Eyed Giant

He landed on something soft – long, thick strands curling round him, like a nest.

A nest of snakes? No. This stuff wasn't smooth, it was hairy. It looked more like ropes. Thick strands of rope leading away down a tunnel in the side of the hole he'd fallen into.

So instead of climbing out of the hole, he did what any boy would do. He followed the ropes down the tunnel to see where it led.

There was light in the tunnel, but it wasn't like day-light or moon-light or candle-light.

The tunnel got wider. He saw grasses growing and trees, too, just like in the world above. But the trees had no leaves and the grass was all dead.

This was a dead world.

So on he walked, and on again.

At last the tunnel opened out into a huge open space. Sitting in the middle was a one-eyed giant. Akim saw the ropes weren't ropes at all, but the giant's hair, all twisted into dread-locks.

"Who are you?" said Akim.

"Who are you?" boomed the giant.

"I asked first," said Akim.

"So you did!" said the giant.

"Now I'm asking you again. Who are you?"

"Don't you know me?" asked the giant.

"No."

"I am Death! I am Death and this is my kingdom. You see this eye of mine?"

"I see it."

"All I have to do is blink – and someone in the world above dies!"

Death blinked and a man appeared, out of nowhere. He looked around but didn't seem to see the giant or the boy. The dead man just wandered off into the shadows.

"You didn't have to do that!" cried Akim.

Death chuckled. "Accidents happen."

"Well, don't do it again," yelled Akim. "I believe you. You're Death."

"And who are you?" said Death.

"I am Akim. I am not afraid of you."

Death frowned. "I am Death! You must be afraid of me."

Akim shook his head. "But I'm not dead. You didn't blink for me, did you? I walked here on my own two feet. Now I'm walking out again."

But he hadn't taken more than a step or two towards the tunnel when one of Death's dread-locks snaked out, tripped him up and carried him back.

"Nobody leaves Death's kingdom," roared Death.

Akim picked himself up and dusted himself down. "I told you, I'm not dead! I don't belong here!"

"But here you are! And here you'll stay," boomed Death.

"I won't."

"You will!"

"Just watch me." Akim set off again towards the tunnel.

But every time he tried to go, one of Death's dread-locks snaked out and carried him back again. Sometimes he was right side up; sometimes upside down, dangling by one foot and dumped on his head.

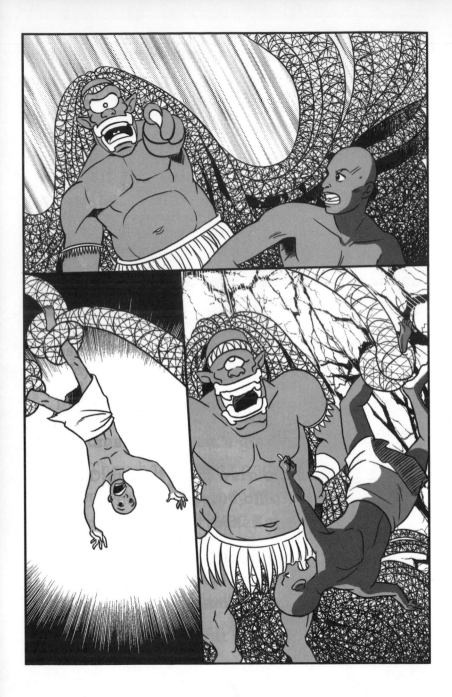

Akim was getting angry. "If only I had my spear!"

"What would you do with it?" said Death.

"I'd fight you! I killed a monster bigger than you!"

"You think you can kill Death?" he laughed.

Akim stamped his foot. "Don't laugh at me!"

"I can't help it. You're funny!" laughed Death.

"I'm not funny!" Akim stamped again. He clenched his fists.

"You are!" said Death.

"I'm not!"

Akim was dancing with rage now.

Death laughed and clapped his hands. "Dance, little man! Dance! Dance!"

"I'm not dancing!" Akim begged.

"Please dance for me."

"No!"

Death laughed so hard he cried. He was holding his sides, tears running down his cheeks. "Stay," said Death. "Please stay. I don't get many laughs down here."

Akim saw he'd never fight his way out of there.

"What will you give me if I stay?" Akim said.

"What do you want?"

"I want a house to live in," said Akim.

"Do you know how to build one?" said Death.

"I know how to build a shelter the way the hunters do. It's a two-man job. You'll have to help. Help me bend these branches over. That's right. Hold them tight while I weave them together at the top. That's right."

"It doesn't look much like a house," said Death.

"It will when we've put a grass roof on it. Help me collect some of this dry grass."

Akim had a plan. So far it was going well. "Can you keep your hair out of the way?" he said. "I keep tripping over it. Coil it over there," he said, "beside our heap of grass. Let's start putting the roof on. You hold each bundle of grass while I tie it in place. Pass me another. Hold it there while I tie it."

"Can I ask a question?" said Death.

"Ask away!" said Akim.

"What are you tying the grass with?"

"Just some old rope I found lying around," said the boy.

"My head itches," said Death.

"Don't let go! You can scratch when we've finished."

A few minutes later – "All done!" said Akim, turning to go.

"Hey!" cried Death. "Where are you going?"

"I'm going home! This time you can't stop me."

Death roared but no dread-locks snaked out to grab Akim. He had used them – every one! – to tie the grass on.

The giant roared louder and tossed his head, but all he did was give himself a head-ache.

Akim was running down the tunnel.

"Come back!" roared Death. "You promised!"

"What did I promise?" Akim called as he ran.

"You said if I helped you build a house you'd stay!"

"I said I needed a house to live in. My house is my home up there in the world of the living!"

Death roared again, louder and longer. The walls of the tunnel began to shake and crumble. The floor heaved like an angry sea. Dust filled the air. But Akim could see the light now at the end of the tunnel.

"Run, run, as fast as you can!" roared Death. "You can't escape Death for ever. You'll be back, boy, sooner than you think! You'll be back!"

Akim's legs were hurting. His lungs were bursting. But if he stopped to rest, he'd be buried alive.

"One day this eye will blink for you!" Death began to laugh again.

Akim was at the bottom of the hole and leaping upwards, fast as a flea, grabbing onto roots and stones to pull himself up. The sides of the hole were crumbling behind him.

He pulled himself up over the edge.

When he looked back the hole had almost vanished.

They'll never believe me, Akim thought, *when I tell them where I've been.*

Chapter 8

You Must Have Been Dreaming

Akim was right. They didn't believe him.

"You must have dreamed it," the villagers said.

"Death's not like that," said his mother. "A one-eyed giant?"

"What is Death like, then?" demanded Akim.

Everyone shook their heads. "We don't know."

"Nobody does. But Death, a one-eyed giant – with dread-locks! I don't think so," said his mother.

"Living at the bottom of that little hole?" said Old Man Misery.

It was no good telling them the hole was deeper when he fell in.

"So where's the rest of it gone?" said Old Man Misery, who knew very well how deep the hole was when he'd dug it.

"Look!" said Abi (remember Abi?). She pointed at the hole. "There's a rock sticking out."

"You must have hit your head when you fell in," said Abi's father. "Got knocked unconscious and dreamed it all."

Maybe he had just dreamed it all.

So why could he still hear Death's laughter in his dreams? Sometimes in the wind or in the sound of water tumbling over rocks, he would hear it. Sometimes he could even make out the words: "One day this eye will blink for you – and you – and you –"

And you!

BATTLE CARDS

Maggie Pearson

Author

Favourite hero:
Dr Who. He uses his brain to get out of trouble.

Favourite monster:
Vampire.

Your weapon of choice:
Kung Fu.

Special secret power:
Being invisible – when all else fails, hide!

Favourite fight scene:
The swordfight at the end of the play 'Hamlet' by Shakespeare. It's best live on stage.

Goodie or baddie:
Goodie. Baddies seem to have all the fun, but they never win.

RELOADED

WHO WILL WIN?

Jotter Studio

Illustrator

Favourite hero:
Prometheus – the Greek hero who first gave fire to man.

Favourite monster:
Werewolf.

Your weapon of choice:
Light saber.

Favourite fight scene:
300 by Frank Miller.

Special secret power:
Taking on other people's secret powers with one touch.

Goodie or baddie:
It depends on the story but I think goodie would be my default setting.

RELOADED

Barrington Stoke would like to thank all its readers for commenting on the manuscript before publication and in particular:

Nick Carton
Darrach Cawley
Jonathan Crook
Jessica Molly Dixon
Iona Hamilton
Katherine McPhie
Neil Musk
Lucy Ann Kennedy Paterson
Liberty Gerrard Pickering
Jake Reynolds
Aidan Sutherland
Aidan Walker
James Woodward

Become a Consultant!

Would you like to give us feedback on our titles before they are published? Contact us at the email address below — we'd love to hear from you!

info@barringtonstoke.co.uk
www.barringtonstoke.co.uk

WANTED: JANOSIK

BY
ANDREW MATTHEWS

Killer. Thief. Outlaw.
And he's the good guy …
Hero to the poor. Hated by the rich.
Wanted: Janosik
Dead Or Alive.

You can order *Wanted: Janosik* directly from
www.barringtonstoke.co.uk

BIMA AND THE WATER OF LIFE

BY
FRANZESKA G. EWART

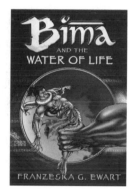

A hero that lives for danger.
An adventure to the ends of the earth.
An evil from the darkest nightmare.
A battle that will go down in history ...
Bima and the Water of Life.

You can order *Bima and the Water of Life* directly from
www.barringtonstoke.co.uk

THE DRAGON AND THE WARLORD

BY
THOMAS BLOOR

Sheng saw Lord Zuko kill his father.
Now the Warlord is destroying everything.
But there's nothing Sheng can do – until he finds
the dragon's pearl.
Revenge is coming. *Watch the skies ...*

You can order *The Dragon and the Warlord* directly from
www.barringtonstoke.co.uk

JACK AND THE DRAGON'S TOOTH

BY
LILY HYDE

Welcome to Jack's world.
Where anything can happen and probably will ...
Starring: a wizard, a dragon and a mouse army!
With bonus FUN and added magic.

You can order *Jack and the Dragon's Tooth* directly from
www.barringtonstoke.co.uk